DUMBO

It was the first day of spring and all the circus animals had received their babies, except for Mrs. Jumbo. Her baby elephant still hadn't arrived.

Later that evening, Mr. Stork landed in the circus train with a very precious bundle.

"It's Jumbo Junior!" the other elephants cried.

When the baby spread out his ears, the elephants couldn't
believe their eyes. They were the biggest ears the elephants had
ever seen! Because of his enormous ears, the other elephants
renamed him Dumbo.

Mrs. Jumbo ignored the taunts of the other elephants. She wrapped her trunk protectively around Dumbo and rocked him to sleep.

Dumbo joined the circus, but he wasn't very well treated.
Sadly, children teased him and grown-ups laughed at him. One day,
some naughty children decided to pull on Dumbo's ears.

Mrs. Jumbo defended her son by standing on her hind legs and scaring the mean children away. When the circus owners saw this, they feared that Mrs. Jumbo might be dangerous and locked her up in a cage.

8

Dumbo was all alone. The other elephants told him that his big ears were an embarrassment to their species. But Timothy the mouse was convinced that one day Dumbo would be a star!

All Dumbo needed was a good circus act, so Timothy concocted a plan. While the ringmaster slept, the mouse snuck into his bedroom and whispered the idea into his ear.

The next day, the ringmaster included Dumbo in a circus act.

Unfortunately, Dumbo wasn't a very good performer.
He tripped over his ears, knocking over the elephant pyramid.

The circus tent collapsed. It was a disaster!

Dumbo was no longer allowed to perform with the elephants and he was forced to join the clown troupe instead.

In Dumbo's new act, he had to leap from the window of a
burning building while clown firefighters put out the fire.
The audience roared with laughter when they saw Dumbo's big ears.

Dumbo was terribly sad. His mother was still caged and he was the outcast of the circus.

"Don't worry, Dumbo," whispered Timothy. "One day, you'll soar above everyone."

That evening, Dumbo dreamed that he was the star of a magic circus. In his dream, he bounced high on a trampoline and flew through the air.

The next morning, Timothy awoke to find five crows staring at him!

"What are you doing up here?" asked the crows.

He suddenly realized that he and Dumbo were in a tree!

"You flew here!" the crows told him.

Dumbo tried to fly, but fell into the water.

"You can do it!" cried Timothy encouragingly.

But no matter how hard Dumbo tried, he couldn't seem to fly again.

The crows took pity on Dumbo. "Use this magic feather," suggested one of the crows. "Hold it tight and it will help you fly!"

Dumbo gripped the magic feather in his trunk and jumped.

Instead of falling, Dumbo was flying!

He soared like an arrow over the hills and trees with the crows by his side.

"We won't tell anyone you can fly!" said Timothy. "We will surprise everyone in the show this afternoon!"

That afternoon, Dumbo prepared for his big act.

"Good luck, Dumbo!" cried Timothy, who was perched in Dumbo's hat.

As Dumbo jumped, he dropped the magic feather! He began to plummet full speed toward the ground.

"It wasn't the feather that made you fly!" the little mouse cried. "You did it on your own!"

Dumbo didn't believe him, but he spread his giant ears and…

… he flew!

Dumbo soared through the air over the astonished crowd. The audience gave Dumbo a standing ovation.

It was an incredible sight to see!

The circus became very popular, all because of Dumbo!
From that day on, Dumbo, his mother, and Timothy traveled all
over the country as the stars of Dumbo's Flying Circus!